Mugs and Rugs

Illustrated by The Artful Doodlers

Random House New York
Thomas the Tank Engine & Friends™

CREATED BY BRITT ALLCROFT

Based on The Railway Series by The Reverend W Awdry. © 2010 Gullane (Thomas) LLC.
Thomas the Tank Engine & Friends and Thomas & Friends are trademarks of Gullane (Thomas) Limited.
HIT and the HIT Entertainment logo are trademarks of HIT Entertainment Limited.

www.stepintoreading.com   www.randomhouse.com/kids   www.thomasandfriends.com

Educators and librarians, for a variety of teaching tools, visit us at
www.randomhouse.com/teachers
ISBN: 978-0-375-85368-5   MANUFACTURED IN CHINA

Bill and Ben.

Bill and Ben meet the men.

The men have a box.

That box is big!

The men lug the box.

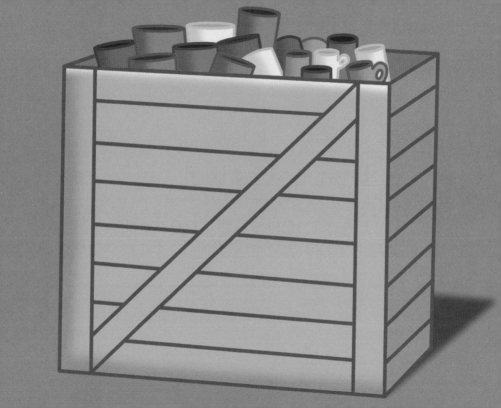

That box has mugs.

That box has rugs.

That box has lots of mugs and rugs.

Can Bill lug that big box?

Bill can not lug that box.

Can Ben lug that big box?

Ben can not lug that box.

The men lug a box to Bill.

Bill has a box of rugs.

The men lug a box to Ben.

Ben has a box of mugs.

Bill and Ben can go!